KT-427-258

Books should be returned or renewed by the
last date stamped above

KEBBE, J

BEG.   -4 AUG 2017

Shredder   25 NOV 2017

or excellence
& Libraries

Kent
County
Council

Shredder

Jonathan Kebbe

Illustrated by Sarah Nayler

SHREDDER
A CORGI PUPS BOOK 0552 551295

Published in Great Britain by Corgi Books,
an imprint of Random House Children's Books

This edition published 2004

1 3 5 7 9 10 8 6 4 2

Typeset in Bembo Schoolbook by Palimpsest Book Production Limited,
Polmont, Stirlingshire

Corgi Books are published by Random House Children's Books,
61–63 Uxbridge Road, London W5 5SA,
a division of The Random House Group Ltd,
in Australia by Random House Australia (Pty) Ltd,
20 Alfred Street, Milsons Point, Sydney, NSW 2061, Australia,
in New Zealand by Random House New Zealand Ltd,
18 Poland Road, Glenfield, Auckland 10, New Zealand,
and in South Africa by Random House (Pty) Ltd,
Endulini, 5A Jubilee Road, Parktown 2193, South Africa

THE RANDOM HOUSE GROUP Limited Reg. No. 954009
www.kidsatrandomhouse.co.uk

A CIP catalogue record for this book
is available from the British Library.

Printed and bound in Great Britain by
Cox & Wyman Ltd, Reading, Berkshire

Contents

Series Reading Consultant: Prue Goodwin,
National Centre for Language and Literacy
University of Reading

Contents

Chapter One

I'm Shredder, the class gerbil.
I'm furry and twitchy and
tame. I'm no bigger than a bar
of soap, and I live in a glass
tank in Miss Kimberly's
classroom.

I'm called Shredder because that's what I do. I shred paper and cardboard with my tiny teeth, filling my home with soft litter. Look closely and you'll see all the tunnels I've made in the litter, and a cosy little nest in the corner.

nest

It gets lonely sometimes. Every morning I run around, hoping to meet another gerbil, but I never do. I get scared too, because Mr Blister, the new headteacher, doesn't like me.

He came in this morning and said to Miss Kimberly, "I wish you'd get rid of that nasty little creature."

Nasty? I'm not nasty.

"Oh I couldn't do that, Mr Blister," whispered Miss Kimberly, who is small and plump and terribly nervous. "The children would be so upset."

"Upset? Nonsense!" said Mr Blister, turning to face the class. All the children shrank in their seats, because Mr Blister looked like the giant in *Jack and the Beanstalk*.

"I like a nice, clean school," he said, smiling sweetly. "And classroom pets are smelly and dirty. This one certainly is," he sniffed.

"Sir, sir, sir!" A boy's hand shot up! It was Dino, a funny, long-haired boy, who's always bringing me seeds to eat. He spends ages standing watching me. He's loud and a little crazy, and no one plays with  him much. I'm his only friend. And now his hand was up.

"You're wrong, sir," he cried.

"Wrong?" boomed Mr Blister.

"Yes, sir!" said Dino. "Shredder's not dirty, he's very clean."

"Clean?"

"He's a desert rat, sir. Desert rats don't need much water, so they hardly ever pee!"

Everyone looked at Dino, amazed.

Mr Blister went off shaking his head and mumbling, "Most peculiar children."

A few minutes later he

marched out into the school garden wearing his wellies and wielding a spade. Whenever he's angry, he digs the heavy soil until the sweat runs down his face. Mr Blister *loves* his garden. It's his favourite place in the whole school.

Phew! I sighed, wiggling my whiskers. I'm safe . . . for the moment.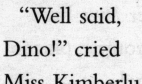

"Well said, Dino!" cried Miss Kimberly. "You're a brave boy."

"A nutter, miss!" someone said.

Children laughed, but Dino wanted to ask a question.

"Miss, does that mean I can take Shredder out and play with him now?"

"Goodness me, no!"

"But, miss—"

"Dino, I keep telling you – if Shredder escaped, Mr Blister would have a fit! We must be very careful. Never take him out on your own again. Is that understood?"

"Yes, miss."

Miss Kimberly returned to her desk.

"Look, children! Remember all those 20ps and 50ps and pound coins you brought in for our seaside trip? Well, I took the bag of coins to the bank, and they exchanged them for ten crisp new ten-pound notes. So now we have ten pounds times ten. And what does that add up to?"

"A million!" cried Dino.

Everybody laughed. Hands
shot up. "One hundred pounds,
miss!"

"Yes! One hundred pounds!"
she announced, waving the
crisp new notes in the air.
"More than enough for a
wonderful day out."

Everyone was excited,
painting pictures of sand castles
and sailboats, and the
fairground they were going
to visit.

Only Dino painted something different – a big picture of *me* shredding a HUGE cornflakes box.

"In a minute I want one of you to take the money to Mr Blister, so he can lock it safely away," said Miss Kimberly.

"Me, miss!' children cried.

But Miss Kimberly chose Dino, because it was break time, and Dino gets lonely at break times. Everyone ran out to play.

"Oh dear, I can't find my envelopes," sighed Miss Kimberly.

"You'll just have to take the money in this," she said, and carefully placed the ten ten-pound notes inside a nearly empty tissue box.

"Miss, first I've got to change
Shredder's water," said Dino.

"No, you can't stay alone in
here."

"It won't take a sec, miss."

"You can do it later."

"But, miss, his water's
disgusting. You *told* us. He has
to have fresh water every single
day."

"All right, but quickly. I'll leave the money in my desk. Change Shredder's water, take the money to Mr Blister and then find me in the playground."

Miss Kimberly put the tissue box in the top drawer of her desk, and carefully closed it.

Chapter Two

As soon as Miss Kimberly had gone, Dino lifted the lid on my tank, unclipped my water bottle and replaced the lid so I couldn't escape. He emptied the stale water and refilled it.

Then he opened the lid on my
tank and replaced the bottle.
The lid was still open. Dino
was looking at me.

"It's not right she won't let
me take you out on my own
any more, Shredder," he said.

He looked out the window. Mr Blister had finished digging and was returning indoors. Miss Kimberly was supervising children in the playground.

I tried to yell – "*Don't do it, Dino! You'll get in trouble.*" But he couldn't hear me. He lifted me out of the tank and rubbed his nose against mine.

"*Shhh*, we don't want to get caught!" he whispered, which was funny, because I didn't make any noise. I only squeak when I get a fright.

He had me on his shoulder. I ran down his arm, over his head, and down the other arm. Up his sleeve I went, and inside his sweater, making

Dino laugh. Then
I was nibbling
his school
tie. I love
shredding
ties. Then he
let me chase a ping-pong ball
on Miss Kimberley's desk.

What fun we were having . . .
until suddenly – someone was
coming!

Squeak! Hide!

It was Miss Kimberly.

"Dino, what's going on?"

"Nothing, miss."

"Are you sure?"

Looking round the room, her eyes fell on my tank. The open lid!

"Where is he?"

"Who, miss?"

"You know who!"

"Um . . . I don't know, miss."

Miss Kimberly looked *very* worried.

"You didn't take him out, Dino, did you?"

Dino lowered his eyes.

"Dino, I'm talking to you. Did you?"

"Yes, miss."

"Well, where is he then?"

"He's . . . he's . . . gone, miss!"

It was true. Miss Kimberly hadn't fully shut the top drawer of her desk, and I squeezed inside. It was nice and dark in there. Even cosier inside the tissue box.

Oh dear, what's happening? Miss Kimberly was running out and calling, "Quickly, children. Shredder's escaped!"

Chapter Three

Clatter-clatter-clatter.

Everyone was running in to look for me.

Squeak-squeak! The fuss was frightening. And when I'm frightened, I grab any paper I find and start shredding – *nip-nip-nip-nip-nip!* I can't help it.

I started to shred the crisp
sheets of paper in the tissue
box, and made myself a nice
little nest of shredded ten-
pound notes. The few
remaining tissues neatly hid
me.

Who's that? Heavy footfalls!
Mr Blister!
"What's going on in here,
Miss Kimberly? Why are your
children crawling round on
their hands and knees?"

Squeak-squeak! My heart was
going to explode!

"They're, um, picking up any
bits of paper they can find,"
replied Miss Kimberly.

"They look as if they're
looking for something."

"No! They're not looking for
anything."

"We're just very tidy kids,
sir!" said Dino.

"Good. That's what I like to
hear," said Mr Blister. "I do like
a nice, clean school."

He marched out again.

Phew! I was safe again.

Or was I?

The search went on. But they still couldn't find me.

"He must have jumped out of the window, miss!" someone called.

I could hear Miss Kimberly telling Dino off. "I told you not to take him out, and now look what you've done!"

The other children were
angry too.

"You've lost Shredder, you
fool, Dino."

"He'll die out there."

"A cat will get him."

"He'll be run over."

Dino didn't answer. Miss Kimberly made everyone work in silence. I lay absolutely still in my new nest. My sharp ears picked up the sound of a boy softly crying.

"Miss," someone called. "Dino's crying."

"What's the matter, Dino?"

"Shredder, miss . . . I only
wanted to stroke him and give
him a bit of fun. Every animal
needs a bit of love. And now
he's going to die and it's all my
fault."

Miss Kimberly tried to
comfort him, but Dino couldn't
stop crying.

I must climb out and show myself, I was thinking, *before poor Dino breaks his heart*. But just as I was about to get out of the box, Miss Kimberly said, "Dino, would you like to take the money down to the office?"

"No, I don't care about the money. I'm never going to the seaside, or anywhere, ever again."

Sniff

"*You* may not care, Dino," said Miss Kimberly, opening the drawer of her desk, "but everyone else is really looking forward to it. Work quietly, everyone. I won't be a minute. I'll leave the classroom door open and just be up the corridor."

Whoops! Lie low! I thought, as the tissue box was lifted out of the drawer with me trembling inside it.

Miss Kimberly carried it out
of the room and down the
corridor. Through a gap in the
box, I saw a door marked
HEADTEACHER'S OFFICE. *Oh no!*

Knock-knock.

"Come in!"

There he was. The giant!
Seated at his desk. He was the
last person I wanted to see!

"Sorry to disturb you, Mr
Blister. This is my seaside trip
money. One hundred pounds.
I'm sorry I couldn't find an
envelope."

"A tissue box! Ah well. As long as the money is safe."

I could feel the box bump down onto the desk. I could hear Miss Kimberly leaving.

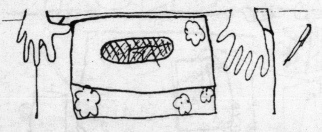

What do I do now?

Whoops! I was flying again. Mr Blister had picked up the box.

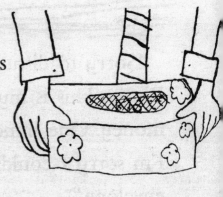

"Better lock this money away," he muttered to himself. The next thing I saw was a big hairy hand reaching under the top layer of tissues to grab me.

I was out in bright light again, trapped in the giant's hand, trying to flatten myself out like a ten-pound note. But Mr Blister stopped suddenly

and stared at what was in his
hand. Not money – but a
desert rat!

"*Ahhhhhhhhhh!*" he
screamed, and threw me into
the air. I hit the ceiling . . . and
then the floor. *Ouch!* My head!
Ouch! My paws!

Quick – *Squeak-squeak!* I was
up the table leg and out
through the open window!

"Miss Kimberly," yelled Mr
Blister. "*MISS KIMBERLY!*"

Chapter Four

My head was still sore. My
heart was sorer still. I hid in
the garden, never stirring
except to hunt for seeds. I
didn't mind being outside, but I
missed my tank. Now I was

missing the children, especially Dino. It had been such fun playing with him. It felt so good when he stroked me.

Climbing up onto the window ledge, I sneaked a look into the classroom as the children arrived back after lunch.

Each girl and boy went straight to my tank, hoping by some miracle I was back. Everyone was upset. Dino's eyes were full of tears.

-sigh-

Mr Blister entered the room. He was holding the tissue box and looking *very* stern. Miss Kimberly was looking *very* nervous. Mr Blister emptied the box onto her desk. The shredded ten-pound notes spilled out in a heap. Goodness me, did I do that?

"Please restore this money to
its former glory, Miss
Kimberly," he said, glaring at
the class. "Let that be a lesson
to you. Never keep nasty
animals!"

He walked out again. Miss Kimberly called Dino up to the front. She was searching in her desk, saying, "I'm sure I had some sticky tape here somewhere."

At afternoon break, I sneaked a look in the staffroom window. Miss Kimberly had ALL the teachers taping scraps of money back together.

At the end of the day I watched the children pack up quietly and go home.

The night set in. I sat very still among Mr Blister's flowers, watching cats and cars come and go. It was no good. I had to do something. I couldn't bear to see Dino's sad face again. Either I left and took my chances with the cats and cars, or . . .

Chapter Five

It was easy stealing back into
the school in the dead of night.
It was harder climbing back
into the tank. Luckily, when I
dashed under the classroom
door and up the table leg, I
found that the lid of my tank

had been carelessly replaced, leaving a squeezing-in gap.

In the morning, when the children arrived, I crawled out of my tunnels and stood up on my hind legs to see who would come in first.

Guess who it was! Dino! He'd come in before the teacher. He looked so sad as he dropped his bag on his chair and came over to the tank. He was looking straight at me. Blinked. Looked away. He couldn't believe it. Looked at me again. His mouth fell open.

He reached over very slowly, lifted the lid. I was in his hands again. He was rubbing my fur gently against his cheek.

Footsteps in the corridor. A
grown-up's footsteps. I felt
Dino's hands tighten around
my bony body.

"What are you doing in here,
Dino? And what have you got
there?"

Dino turned slowly.

"A gerbil?"
said Miss
Kimberly.
"You've
got a new
one?"

"No, miss.
It's Shredder."

"You found him!"

"No, miss. He came back by himself. He *loves* it here."

A shadow fell across the room. Mr Blister! He stared at me.

"I *was* about to deliver some good news," he said. "The bank has kindly  agreed to replace the patched-up notes with new ones."

The other children were coming in now. They looked at Mr Blister. They saw Dino

holding me and whispered to each other.

"Is it a new gerbil?"

"No, it's Shredder. He's come back."

Children were moving carefully round Mr Blister, coming to make sure it really

was me. They all looked at
each other.

Mr Blister took a huge step
towards us. Everyone froze.

"After that creature shredded
up all your money, I'm
surprised you children still want
to keep him. What use is he?"

Dino looked up at him. "Sir! Guess what? My dad says shredded paper is good for compost heaps, and what your garden needs is a compost heap. Just think of all the waste paper and cardboard Shredder could shred for you. Shredder's not a pest, sir. He's a hard worker. And guess what, sir? We wouldn't charge you a penny!"

Mr Blister's eyebrows swooped like eagles. Was he going to go mad?

No! A smile broke across his face.

"*Hmmm*," he rumbled, rubbing his chin. "I'll have to think about it."

After he had gone, Miss Kimberly gave Dino *two* excited thumbs up!

Dino kissed me, and everyone crowded round to stroke me.

"Welcome back, Shredder!"

They slapped Dino on the back.

"Well done, Dino, you're brilliant!"

Miss Kimberly tapped her desk. "Come on, children. Books out."

With a HUGE HAPPY SMILE Dino put me back in my tank.

I'm home.

THE END